✳ Summer Fun ✳

By the Same Author

Published by Harcourt Brace Jovanovich, Inc.

Penny and Peter   1946
Betsy and the Boys   1945
Here's a Penny   1944
Back to School with Betsy   1943
Primrose Day   1942
Betsy and Billy   1941
Two and Two are Four   1940
"B" Is For Betsy   1939

Published by William Morrow & Company

Happy Birthday From Carolyn Haywood   1984
Santa Claus Forever!   1983
Halloween Treats   1981
The King's Monster   1980
Eddie's Menagerie   1978
Betsy's Play School   1977
A Valentine Fantasy   1976
Eddie's Valuable Property   1975
"C" Is for Cupcake   1974
Away Went the Balloons   1973
A Christmas Fantasy   1972
Eddie's Happenings   1971
Merry Christmas from Betsy   1970
Taffy and Melissa Molasses   1969
Ever-Ready Eddie   1968
Betsy and Mr. Kilpatrick   1967
Eddie the Dog Holder   1966
Robert Rows the River   1965
Eddie's Green Thumb   1964
Here Comes the Bus!   1963
Snowbound with Betsy   1962

SUMMER FUN

Carolyn Haywood

Illustrated by Julie Durrell

* *

William Morrow and Company, Inc. New York

1 2 3 4 5 6 7 8 9 10

Library of Congress Cataloging-in-Publication Data
Haywood, Carolyn, 1898–
Summer fun.
Summary: A collection of ten stories, five previously published
by the author, all of which take place during
the summer.
1. Children's stories, American. [1. Summer—
Fiction. 2. Short stories] I. Durrell, Julie, ill.
II. Title.
PZ7.H31496Su 1986   [E]   85-25864
ISBN 0-688-04958-3

5/93 13186407

Dedicated with love
to the memory of
ELISABETH BEVIER HAMILTON, my first editor

The author expresses appreciation to Leslie Wylie, whose son, Aaron, won the Hermit Crab Race at Ocean City, New Jersey in 1983, for sharing her knowledge of hermit crabs.

✻ Contents ✻

· I ·

Bears and Blueberries

Peter was spending his summer vacation at a boys' camp. The camp was on a lake where the boys swam and sailed. Beyond the lake there was a mountain, and from time to time the boys went on camping trips to the mountain.

Peter had made two good friends among the boys who shared his cabin, Steve and Don. The group that shared the cabin was called the Beavers. All together there were five groups, each with two counselors.

Today they were all going up to the mountain, where they would be spending the night. They were going in trucks part way, and the rest of the way on foot. Mr. Jones and Woodie, the counselors for the Beavers, were going with them. Woodie was a great favorite with all of the boys because he had lived all his life on the edge of the woods. He knew everything about the woods, the trees, the wild-flowers, the animals and birds. He knew all of the trails. In fact, he knew so much about the woods that they called him Woodie.

Each group had its own equipment: pup tents in which to sleep, kettles for soup and cocoa, quarts of milk in thermos containers, and best of all, hamburger packed in dry ice.

It was a beautiful, warm day. Great piles of billowy white clouds floated in the clear blue sky. The boys climbed into the trucks and rattled off over the country roads until they reached the spot from which they would start their hike.

The five groups were going by different trails. They would meet at the top of the mountain. There the truck with the food and the pup tents would be waiting for them, and there they would spend the night.

Peter's group of eight boys, with Woodie at the head of the line and Mr. Jones at the end, struck off through the woods. Steve, like Woodie and Mr. Jones, was carrying a hatchet, for the most skillful boys were permitted to carry them. Steve felt very proud to be one of these boys, for he was the youngest ever to pass the hatchet test.

Woodie was taking them up a pretty steep trail. It was a stiff climb. Every once in a while Steve would have to help Woodie and Mr. Jones hack away the underbrush so that they could all get through.

Finally they came into a clearing. It was a long slope, and Woodie pointed out to the boys that at one time it had probably been a ski slope, but now it was covered with blueberries.

"Hey, guys!" cried Steve. "Here's where we get blueberries! Look at 'em.

Immediately every boy set to work to gather blueberries in his tin cup. Some of the boys gradually worked up the slope, others worked across. Peter and Steve and Don, without realizing it, were working down. They had never seen such big berries or so many of them. But their cups didn't fill very rapidly, because they ate two to each one they dropped into their cups. Before long the three boys had worked their way behind a clump of spruce trees. They stood up and looked around. The two counselors and the rest of the boys were out of sight. Peter and Steve and Don seemed to be alone on the mountainside. But just then Peter saw a man farther down the mountain. The man was leaning over, picking blueberries.

"There's a man down there," said Peter. "I guess he's picking blueberries, too."

"Hey, guys!" said Steve. "Maybe that man lives near here and maybe he knows someone who would bake us some pies."

"We haven't time to wait around here while someone bakes us some pies," said Peter.

"We could pick them up tomorrow, on our way back," said Steve.

"Sure we could," said Don. "Let's go ask him about it."

The boys started off on a quick run down the slope toward the man. But they hadn't run very far when the man straightened up and looked right at them. The boys stopped in their tracks. To their amazement it wasn't a man at all. It was a big black bear! As soon as the bear saw the boys he began to run and it looked as though he were running right toward them.

The three boys turned on their heels and ran back up the slope as fast as their legs would carry them. Their blueberries flew right and left. Once around the clump of trees they could see the other boys, Mr. Jones, and Woodie. Don, who was little, ran right to Woodie and climbed up his legs just as though he were climbing a pole. Peter and Steve kept right on going. As they passed Mr. Jones and the boys, they cried, "It's a bear! It's a bear!"

The five other boys joined Peter and Steve and they all went tearing up the mountain in a shower of blueberries.

"Hey! Come back!" Mr. Jones called after them. But the boys didn't stop running until they ran out of breath. Then they looked back. They could see only Mr. Jones, Woodie, and Don, who was still clinging to Woodie's legs. The bear was nowhere in sight.

The truth was that the bear had been just as frightened as the boys, and he had made for the woods, lickety-split.

When their breath returned, the boys set to work picking more blueberries.

"If we spend any more time picking blueberries," said Mr. Jones, "we won't get to the top of the mountain tonight."

"It looks to me as though we're going to have a shower," said Woodie, looking at the dark clouds that were gathering in the west. "Come on! Let's push ahead."

The boys fell into line behind Woodie, and they started off again on the trail. Every once in a while there was a distant roll of thunder.

"I wonder whether we will get that storm," said Mr. Jones.

"Seems to be coming in our direction," said Woodie.

The thunder grew louder and the woods grew darker. The wind blew the tops of the trees, and dead branches cracked off and fell to the ground. Then it began to rain in great big drops. No sooner had the boys put on their ponchos than it began coming down in torrents. The woods protected them a little, but soon they came out into a clearing. And there, before their eyes, was an old lumber camp with a log cabin.

"Well, this is fortunate," said Mr. Jones. "This belongs to the Pontiac Lumber Company. We can go into this cabin if it's open."

Mr. Jones pushed against the door and it opened. "I'll go in first," he said, "and see if there are any little porcupines living here. We don't want to get into trouble with those little beggars."

Mr. Jones pushed the door open and flashed his pocket light around. Sure enough, there were two porcupines, one in each corner, with their faces turned in and their tails out. They looked like naughty boys who had been stood in the corner. But Mr. Jones knew porcupines. He knew why they had run into the corners. A corner was the safest spot. Their tails, their only weapon, could stick out. Now they were switching them, back and forth, ready to give anyone who came too close a wicked slap.

Mr. Jones came outside. "Sure enough!" he said. "There are two porkies. They have run into the corners and we'll have to find a way to get rid of them."

"Can't you hit them with an axe?" one of the boys asked. "That would kill them, wouldn't it?"

"Kill them!" Woodie cried. "We don't kill the little animals in the woods. They haven't done anything to us. We probably look like an army of giants to them, and they are scared. We just have to find a way to get rid of them without hurting them. After all, they don't mind the rain, but we do.

"Porcupines are not very bright creatures,"

7

Woodie continued. "There is an old legend about why the porcupine hasn't much sense. I'll tell it to you sometime."

While Woodie was saying this, he was examining some pieces of saplings that were lying near the cabin.

"Will you tell us the story tonight?" Peter asked, as he huddled with the rest of the boys against the side of the cabin.

"Remind me and I will tell it to you," Woodie replied.

In a few minutes Woodie had found two long pieces of sapling, about the same length and very straight. The boys watched him as he tied the two pieces together with a handkerchief that he had taken off of his neck. When he had finished, they looked like an enormous pair of pliers.

As Woodie walked into the cabin he said, "Now everyone stand away from the door and back against the wall. I'm going to bring out a porcupine."

Woodie advanced to one corner. He reached out with the big pliers and very carefully picked up one porcupine and carried it outside. He took it quite a long way from the cabin and set it down. All the time the porcupine was slapping its tail, but it

didn't touch Woodie because the wooden pliers were so very long.

Then Woodie returned for the second one. All the boys were holding their breath, and when Woodie finally deposited the second porcupine beside its brother everyone breathed again. Then the boys went into the cabin. They took off their ponchos. They took off their shoes and changed their socks. Mr. Jones lit some candles and Woodie made a fire in the stove.

"Woodie, will you tell us the porcupine story now?" said Steve.

"When I get this fire burning I will," Woodie replied.

Soon there was a good fire burning, and the boys sat around on the floor eating chocolate bars, and Woodie began.

"This is an Indian legend. In the beginning, when the Great Spirit had made the world and the mighty Indian, he sat down outside of his wigwam to rest. The world was very beautiful and the Indian was very strong. The Great Spirit thought that they were very good. But the Great Spirit was not satisfied. He felt that something more was needed. He thought and thought, and then it came to him

that what the world needed was animals. All kinds
of animals. So the Great Spirit got up and went
out to look for some very fine clay. When he found
it, he carried it into his wigwam. There he mixed
the clay with magic and, one by one, he made the
animals. He made them all different and some were
very fair to look upon. There were times when the
Great Spirit ran short of magic, and then the animals looked just a little queer. But the Great Spirit
liked all of them, even queer-looking ones like the
platypus. There were a few, like the crocodile and
the anteater, that puzzled the Great Spirit, and he
wondered whether he had gotten any magic at all
into them. But he said to himself, 'Well, their
mothers will love them.'

"But after he had finished all of the animals, he
looked at them, and even though he had made
them, he had to admit that there was a little
something the matter with all of them.

"The Great Spirit sat deep in thought. At last
he said to himself, 'I know what is the matter with
the animals! They need brains.' The Great Spirit
knew that it would be very difficult to make brains
for the animals. It would take much, much magic,
but the Great Spirit knew that it must be done,

11

that the animals must have brains and that he would have to make them.

"So the Great Spirit went out and found himself a gourd. Then he made himself a beautiful wooden spoon. The Great Spirit worked all night long with deep, deep magic, and when the sun rose he had a gourd filled with brains for the animals. He dipped his wooden spoon into the gourd and gave each animal a portion. To the horse and the dog and the bear he gave each a large spoonful. And he patted each one on the head as he let it go. When he came to the fox the Great Spirit's hand slipped and he gave the fox too much. But he patted it on the head and let it go off into the forest. There was very little left in the gourd when the mice and the chipmunk came for their portions, and when the little field mouse came, the Great Spirit had to scrape and scrape and scrape the gourd to get a tiny speck of brains. But the field mouse went away looking pleased. The gourd was clean and shiny when the Great Spirit put it away.

"The Great Spirit wiped his hands and sat down outside his wigwam to rest and to enjoy the works of his hands, for the Great Spirit thought that they were very good indeed. He had been enjoying their goodness for some time when he chanced to look down at his feet, and there stood a little animal who hadn't been given any brains at all. The Great Spirit knew the awful fact that there was none to give the little animal. Not even a crumb. But the Great Spirit knew that he had to do something for the little animal, so he walked into the woods to see if he could find something that he could give it. The Great Spirit hunted and hunted and finally he came to a thorn tree. He picked thorns off the tree and, one by one, the Great Spirit gave the little porcupine quills, instead of brains."

When Woodie had finished his story, the rain had lessened. But now the boys were hungry. All the fresh milk had gone off in the truck to the top of the mountain, but fortunately Mr. Jones found a package of powdered milk and a box of oatmeal in his duffel bag, and with some nearby spring water he made a gallon of milk. Soon the boys were eating the oatmeal and drinking steaming cups of cocoa.

By the time they had finished their supper, the rain had stopped altogether, but it was beginning to get dark.

"I think we had better spend the night in the cabin," said Mr. Jones. "We can't possibly get to the top of the mountain before dark. We have our sleeping bags so we'll just hole up here. The lumbermen are all friends of the camp director, Mr. Sherwood, and they'd be glad to let us stay here."

The boys were tired and glad to lie down.

Mr. Jones slept right by the door.

The rain clouds had rolled away and left a beautiful star-filled sky. When Woodie saw the lovely sky, he decided to sleep out under the stars, so he climbed out of the window onto the flat roof of a shed. Here he made his bed.

Before long everyone was sound asleep, but in the middle of the night Woodie woke up. It had turned very cold. He decided to go inside the cabin with the boys. He got up and crawled to the window, dragging his sleeping bag behind him. Just as he poked his head and shoulders through the window, Peter woke up. He peered into the darkness. He saw a great dark creature coming through the window. Peter let out a piercing scream.

"Bears!" he yelled, leaping from his bed. "Bears!"

With this, all of the boys awoke. They crawled out of their sleeping bags and rushed after Peter out the door. Eight pairs of feet had stepped all over Mr. Jones before he knew what had happened.

"Come back!" cried Woodie.

"Come back!" shouted Mr. Jones. "Come back. It's only Woodie!"

"It was too cold out there on the roof, even in my sleeping bag," said Woodie. "I had to come inside."

When the excitement was over and they had all settled down again, Mr. Jones said, "I would just like to know which of you fellows stepped on my face."

"I guess I did," said Steve. "Feels as though something bit my toe."

2

The Watermelon Party

One evening Betsy and her father were sitting in the summerhouse in the garden. Her father was reading the paper, and Betsy was pasting stamps in her album. When it grew too dark to see clearly, her father laid his paper aside and said, "Time to stop, Betsy."

"I've finished," said Betsy, getting up from the table. "Look, Daddy. Look at this beautiful stamp from Japan. Billy Porter gave it to me. I gave him one that came from Egypt for it."

Betsy carried her stamp album to her father. He looked at the stamp and said, "That surely is a nice one." Betsy sat down on her father's lap. "My goodness, Betsy," he said, "You're getting too big to sit on my lap. Look where your legs come. Dangling way down like macaroni."

Betsy laughed. "I'm never going to be too big to sit on your lap, Daddy," she said.

"Then I'm going to have to grow bigger," said her father.

Betsy leaned her head against her father's and said, "Tell me about when you played in your grandfather's summerhouse."

"I think I've told you everything," her father replied.

"Think," insisted Betsy.

Father thought for a few minutes, and then he said, "Did I ever tell you about the watermelon parties we used to have?"

"Watermelon parties!" exclaimed Betsy. "You never told me! What's a watermelon party?"

"It's a party where you eat watermelon and plenty of it. You try to keep all of your seeds, because there's a prize that goes to the one who has the most seeds at the end of the party."

"Did you have the party outdoors?" asked Betsy.

"Oh, yes," her father replied, "and always in the evening. The summerhouse was the headquarters for the watermelons. That's where Grandfather cut them."

"I guess you have to have a watermelon party

outdoors," said Betsy. "I guess it's pretty sloppy."

Her father laughed. "Sloppy is a very good word for a watermelon party."

"How could you see to get the seeds out?" asked Betsy.

"We had paper lanterns strung all around on wires. It was a pretty sight."

"I wish I could have a watermelon party," said Betsy. "Do you think I could?"

"I don't see why not," her father replied. "But we ought to have paper lanterns. I can't imagine a watermelon party without paper lanterns."

"What happened to the ones your grandfather had?"

"I've no idea," said her father. "Perhaps they're packed away in your grandmother's attic. We could write and ask her."

"Oh, let's!" said Betsy. "Let's go in and write her now."

On Saturday morning the parcel-post truck stopped at Betsy's house. The driver jumped down and lifted a big parcel out of the truck. Betsy and her sister, Star, came running from the summer-house to see what was in the parcel. As soon as her mother looked at it, she said, "It's from

Grandma. It must be the paper lanterns."

"Oh, open it, Mom!" said Betsy. "Let's see!"

Her mother cut the heavy cord on the parcel and pulled off the paper. Inside there was a cardboard carton. She lifted the flaps and took out some crumpled-up newspaper. Star and Betsy knelt on the floor beside their mother and watched the unpacking. "Oh!" cried Star. "They're not lanterns. They're just flat hats."

"They are lanterns," her mother laughed, shaking one out.

As it dropped open, the children saw that it really was a lantern. It was a beautiful one, made of oiled paper stretched over very thin bamboo hoops. It was decorated with pink and red flowers with green leaves. Star and Betsy watched as their mother removed each lantern. There were twenty-five of them and every one was beautiful. In the bottom of each one there was a place for a candle.

"Oh, Mom!" cried Betsy. "I can't wait to see them all lighted."

"Is it going to be Betsy's party or my party?" asked Star.

"It's going to be Betsy's party," her mother replied. "You don't have your parties in the evening. You have them in the afternoon."

"But I can come to Betsy's party, can't I?"

"If you can stay awake," said her mother.

"How many friends can I invite?" Betsy asked.

"Ask all of your friends who haven't gone away," said her mother.

"Shall I ask those new boys who just moved in next door to Billy Porter?" asked Betsy.

"Yes," replied her mother. "Mrs. Porter says they're nice boys."

"Jack is going to be in my class in school," said Betsy, "and Billy says little Rodney's always up to something."

"Are the Wilson boys home?" asked Betsy's mother.

"Eddie is," said Betsy. "The twins went to camp, and Rudy is helping on his grandfather's farm. I'll invite Eddie."

Betsy lost no time spreading the news that she was having a watermelon party the following Saturday evening. As soon as Eddie Wilson heard of it, he came riding over on his bicycle to find out everything about the watermelon party. He found Betsy and Star in the summerhouse.

"Hi, Betsy," he said. "What are we going to do at your watermelon party?"

"We're going to eat watermelon," said Betsy.

"Sounds good," said Eddie.

"And everybody is going to count their seeds, and the one who has the most seeds after we're through eating watermelon will get a prize," said Betsy.

"How many pieces of watermelon do we get?" Eddie asked.

"As much as we want," said Betsy. "My father is going to get lots and lots of watermelons."

"Well, I can eat a lot of watermelon," said Eddie.

On his way home, Eddie passed this news on to his new friend Rodney. "I'll get the prize," said Eddie.

"How do you know you will?" asked Rodney.

" 'Cause I can eat more watermelon than anybody," said Eddie. "So I'll get the most seeds. It's simple."

When Eddie left, Rodney thought to himself, That Eddie Wilson is very cocky. Rodney thought about Eddie's boasting a long time. By afternoon he had decided upon a plan. He said to his mother, "Couldn't we have watermelon for dessert tonight?"

"If you want watermelon," his mother replied, "you go to the store on your bike and get one."

Rodney set off with the money that his mother had given him. When he reached the store he looked over the watermelons. "I'll take that one," he said to the storekeeper, pointing to the biggest one in the lot. Rodney handed his money to the man, and as the man gave him his change, Rodney said, "Do you think there are a lot of seeds in that watermelon?"

"I guess there are a good many," said the man.

Rodney couldn't lift the watermelon to put it in the basket on his bicycle. The storekeeper had to put it in for him. When he reached home, his mother had to help him carry it into the kitchen. Then she had to take almost everything out of the refrigerator in order to get the watermelon in.

When the watermelon was served at dinner, Jack and his father both said, "Oh, good! Watermelon!"

When dinner was over, Rodney said, "I'll help you clear the table, Mom." He carried the dessert plates out to the kitchen very carefully. "Mom," he said, "don't throw the seeds away. I want them."

"All of them?" asked his mother.

"Yes, all of them," replied Rodney.

"Whatever do you want with watermelon seeds?" his mother asked.

"I'm collecting them," said Rodney.

"You do collect the strangest things," said his mother, as she watched Rodney dropping seeds into a jar.

As soon as all of the big watermelon had been eaten, Rodney persuaded his mother to let him go to the store for another one. By Thursday night everyone was fed up with watermelon except Rodney. "I don't want to see another piece of watermelon for a month," said his father.

"Betsy is having a watermelon party on Saturday night," said Rodney.

"I'm glad I'm not invited," said his father.

"What do we do at a watermelon party?" asked Jack.

"Eat watermelon, of course," said Rodney.

"What else do we do?" asked his brother.

"You'll find out," said Rodney.

Every evening Rodney carried the dishes from

the dinner table, gathered up all the watermelon seeds, and put them in his jar. By Friday he had a half-pint jar filled with black seeds. Rodney felt that whatever the prize at Betsy's party was going to be, it was already his.

On Saturday afternoon Rodney began to wonder how he could carry his watermelon seeds to the party without letting anyone see them. He decided to put them in a paper bag. He planned to stuff the bag of seeds into his pocket. He poured them from the jar into the paper bag and stood the bag on the windowsill in his bedroom. The damp seeds began to make a wet spot on the bottom of the paper bag.

When it was time for him and his brother Jack to leave for the party, Rodney picked up the paper bag. To his surprise, the bottom of the bag broke and the seeds fell to the floor in a shower. Rodney dropped down on his hands and knees and began picking up the slippery seeds.

Rodney's father was going to drive the boys over to Betsy's house. Jack and his father were already in the car. "Hey, Rodney," Jack called, "get a move on. Eddie's here. We're ready to go."

❋ The Watermelon Party ❋

"I'm coming," Rodney called back, as he crawled around the floor.

In a minute he heard Jack shout again, "So long, Rodney, we're going."

"Half a minute and we're leaving," his father called out.

The faster Rodney tried to pick up the seeds, the more they slipped out of his fingers. He did not have anything to put them in, so he put them in his pocket. He was gathering up the ones that had rolled under the bed, when his father called out, "Time's up, Rodney. You can walk."

Before Rodney could get out from under the bed, he heard the car drive off. He scrambled to his feet and decided to leave the rest of the seeds where they were. Most of them were in his pocket. He dashed downstairs and ran up the street. He thought maybe his father would be waiting for him around the corner. But when he turned the corner the car was out of sight. Rodney settled down to a fast trot. He held his hand over his pocket so that the seeds would not spill out.

It was a long way to Betsy's house, and now it seemed longer than ever. He could feel his legs moving, but he did not seem to be getting to Betsy's very fast. At last he reached Betsy's corner and turned into the street. Rodney could see a soft light shining out into the darkness of the street, but it was not until he reached the front gate that he saw what was making the light. Strung all over the yard, from tree to tree, were beautiful paper lanterns. Rodney thought he had never seen anything nicer than those lanterns. He ran the rest of the way. By the time he arrived, everyone was eating a piece of watermelon. "Hello, Rodney," Betsy called out when she saw him. "Come and get your watermelon from my father. He's over in the summerhouse."

Rodney went to the summerhouse. "Hello, young fellow!" said Betsy's father. "Here, take this piece." He handed Rodney a large paper plate with a big chunk of red, ripe watermelon on it.

Rodney looked at it. Then he said, "This piece doesn't have any black seeds. Can I have a piece with black seeds, please?"

"Sorry, son," said Betsy's father, "but these watermelons all have white seeds."

"No black seeds at all?" exclaimed Rodney.

"Not a one," said Betsy's father.

Rodney sat down with his piece of watermelon.

He ate a few bites. He could hear Eddie Wilson say, "Oh, boy! Look at all these seeds. I'm ready for another piece."

"Never heard of watermelons with white seeds," Rodney muttered to himself. He took another bite. It was good watermelon, but somehow he had lost his appetite for watermelon. He watched the other children going to and from the summerhouse with their plates. He heard them shout to each other about the number of seeds that they were collecting. At last all the watermelon had been eaten, and the children laughed and squealed as they counted their slippery seeds.

"These white seeds are so little," said Ellen.

"Yes, they're harder to count than the big black ones," said Betsy.

Rodney just stood watching. He felt like an outsider, and he did not even bother to count the few white seeds that had come out of his piece of watermelon. He could feel the lump in his pocket made by the black seeds he had brought to the party. A whole pocketful, and they were no good! Rodney did not feel any better when he saw the prize that Eddie Wilson won—a beautiful little sailboat painted bright red. The inside was light blue. Ellen won second prize. It was a rainbow kite.

The children played games, but Rodney spent his evening kicking a stone up and down the garden path. He never looked up at the paper lanterns. He didn't see the tiny lanterns of fireflies twinkling in the bushes. He didn't smell the honeysuckle. He just kicked a stone.

Rodney was glad when the party was over and his father came to take them home. When he reached home he went right up to his room. As he walked through the door, he slipped on a watermelon seed. Down he went and bumped his nose. He began to cry. He sat on the floor and rubbed his nose, while the tears ran down his cheeks. In a few moments he got up, reached into his pocket, and pulled out a handful of watermelon seeds. He dropped them into the wastepaper basket and said, "I hate watermelons!" Then he sobbed, and called, "Mom!"

His mother came upstairs. "What's the matter, dear?" she asked.

"I fell down and bumped my nose," Rodney said.

His mother put her arm around him, and said, "Let me look at it." Rodney lifted his face to his mother. It was wet with tears, sticky from watermelon seeds, and very dirty. "There isn't anything the matter with your nose, son," said his mother. "It's just dirty." Rodney cried harder. "Oh, Rodney, didn't you have a good time at the party?" she asked.

"No!" sobbed Rodney. Then he told his mother the whole story about the watermelon seeds.

When he finished his mother held him tight, and said, "I'm glad you told me, Rodney. I don't believe you'll ever do anything like that again."

Rodney gulped. Then he said, "I'm sort of hungry."

"What would you like to eat?" asked his mother.

Rodney looked up at his mother, and said, "You don't happen to have a piece of watermelon in the refrigerator, do you?"

"I'll go see," said his mother.

· 3 ·

A Bell for Jim Dandy

One afternoon Billy Porter was roller-skating on the sidewalk in front of his house when the Jim Dandy truck came up the street. The Jim Dandy truck sold Jim Dandies—ice cream on a stick. There were a great many different kinds of Jim Dandies. There was vanilla covered with chocolate, vanilla covered with nuts, vanilla covered with coconut. There was also chocolate ice cream covered with the same coatings. There were peach and strawberry Jim Dandies, and there were others made of orange ice and raspberry ice. These melted quickly, but they were pretty to look at. All the different kinds were kept frozen as hard as bricks inside of the truck. When the driver took them out, they smoked as they struck the warm air. All the children liked to buy Jim Dandies.

The driver of the truck was always called Jim. This summer one of the high-school boys was driving the truck. His name was Doremus Freemantle, and he liked being called Jim for a change.

Billy watched the white truck as it drew nearer, wondering why he couldn't hear the bell ring. Usually he knew that the truck was in the neighborhood long before he saw it because of the bell that rang every few seconds. He wished he had the money to buy a Jim Dandy, but he had spent his whole week's allowance on a toy airplane that he had seen in a shop window a few days ago. The airplane was broken now, and Billy wished he had the money he had spent for it. I could have bought a Jim Dandy, thought Billy, if only I hadn't spent all my money.

The truck went very slowly. To Billy's surprise, he heard Jim shouting, "Jim Dandies! Jim Dandies!" But no one came running out of the houses, the way they usually did, to buy any. Billy skated toward the truck. "Hi!" he shouted.

"Hi, Billy," Jim called back.

"Why don't you ring your bell?" Billy asked.

"It doesn't work," Jim answered. "I don't know what's the matter with it."

"Oh, that's too bad," said Billy.

"Yeah," said Jim. "Haven't had many customers, and I'm hoarse as an old bullfrog from shouting."

"Maybe I can help you," said Billy. "We have a bell. I'll see if I can find it." Billy started for his house. Then an idea came to him. He turned around and skated back to the truck. "Jim," he called out, "if I can find the bell would you let me come along to ring it?"

"Sure!" replied Jim. "I'll even pay you."

Billy's face lit up like a lamp. "You will?" he said. "How much?"

"I'll give you a Jim Dandy," replied Jim. "Any flavor you want."

"Oh! That great!" said Billy. "I'll take a chocolate one covered with chocolate." Then he said, "No, that chocolate's very thin. I'll take a chocolate covered with nuts."

"Nothing doing yet," said Jim. "You get the bell first and do a little work. You're not going to get paid in advance."

"Okay," said Billy. "I'll be right back." He skated off at top speed. At his front door he quickly unfastened his skates. "Mom!" he shouted. "Mom!"

"What do you want?" his mother called back.

Billy rushed upstairs to his mother. "Oh, Mom!" he said. "I've got a job! Where's our old bell?"

"What kind of a job do you have?" Mrs. Porter asked.

"I'm going to ring the bell for the Jim Dandy truck," said Billy. "Only I have to find a bell, 'cause Jim's bell is broken. Do you know where that bell is that was around here, Mom?"

"I haven't seen it for ages," said his mother.

"Well, will you help me find it, please?" Billy began looking on top of every table and chest and on every shelf. His mother pulled out drawers. They couldn't find the bell. Billy stopped hunting for a moment and looked out of the window. The truck was waiting right in front of the house. Billy ran into his own room. "I have to find it," he called to his mother. "I'll get a nice ride, and I'm going to get paid, too. I'm going to get a chocolate Jim Dandy with nuts."

Just then Jim bellowed from out front, "Hey, Billy! Get a move on. I can't wait all day."

"I'm coming," Billy shouted back from the front window.

"Billy," said his mother, "I haven't seen that bell for a long time. I think it may have been thrown away."

"Oh, Mom!" said Billy. "That's awful!" Then he said, "Well, maybe I could take my flute. Do you think the flute would be all right?"

His mother looked very doubtful. "I don't think you can play a flute on an ice-cream truck," she said.

"Well, what about my drum?" he said.

"Hey, Billy!" came from out front. "I'm going on."

Billy picked up his flute in one hand and his drum in the other and dashed down the stairs. The screen door banged behind him as he ran out to the truck. "I couldn't find the bell," he called to Jim. "But I've got my flute and my drum."

"Flute!" cried Jim. "Who do you think I am, the Pied Piper?"

Billy hadn't thought of the Pied Piper, but now that Jim had mentioned him, Billy remembered the old story. "Why not?" said Billy. "All the children ran after the Pied Piper. You want the children to run after you, don't you?"

"Come along," said Jim, with a sigh. "Step lively. But don't forget it was rats that came out first. I don't want a gang of rats running after the Jim Dandy truck." He reached down and took the drum out of Billy's hand. Then Billy climbed into the seat beside Jim.

"What should I play?" asked Billy.

"What can you play?" said Jim.

"I can play 'Way Down upon the Swanee River,' " said Billy.

"That ought to make everybody jump," said Jim. "Anything else?"

"How about 'Little Drops of Water, Little Grains of Sand'?" asked Billy. "I just learned that."

"Won't do," Jim told him. "Everybody would think it was raining and go rushing for their umbrellas."

"Well, I can play 'Now the Day is Over,' " said Billy. "Only I don't play that so well."

"Skip it!" said Jim. "I have to sell a lot of Jim Dandies before this day is over."

"Oh," said Billy. "Well, how about 'Yankee Doodle'?"

36

"That's more like it," said Jim.

Billy put his flute to his lips and began to play "Yankee Doodle." He played it through twice. Then he said, "Anybody coming?"

"Not a soul," said Jim. Then he looked back. "Not even one rat."

"Should I try the drum?" Billy asked.

"Well, it won't make things any worse," said Jim.

Billy laid his flute on the seat beside him and picked up his drum. He pulled the sticks out of the bands that held them fast to the drum and began to beat out a rhythm. After a minute or two he called, "See anybody coming?"

"What did you say?" Jim shouted back.

"I said do you see anybody coming?" Billy yelled, beating on the drum.

"No," shouted Jim.

"I'll do it harder," Billy screamed. He beat the drum until he was red in the face. "When do I get my chocolate Jim Dandy with nuts?" he yelled.

"Not until we get a customer," Jim shouted at the top of his lungs.

Now the truck had turned into the street where Betsy lived. It rolled along slowly under the trees. Suddenly Billy had an idea. He stopped beating the drum and said, "Jim, stop right up there just beyond the hydrant."

"Now what?" said Jim.

"Well, I have a friend who lives there," said Billy, "and I think maybe she has a bell."

Jim stopped in front of Betsy's house, and Billy jumped down. "Make it snappy," said Jim. "And don't come back with a violin."

"I'll be right back," said Billy.

Betsy and Star were playing in the summer-house. They were surprised to see Billy. He ran up to them all out of breath. "Say, Betsy," he said, "have you got a bell?"

"A what?" said Betsy.

"A bell," said Billy. "You know, that you ring."

"Oh! A bell!" said Betsy. "What for?"

"Listen, Betsy, we're in a big hurry," said Billy. "I'm helping Jim, and his bell is broken, and all I have is my flute and my drum, and they don't do any good."

Betsy looked puzzled. "What don't they do?" she asked.

"They don't bring the customers out, stupid," said Billy. "The customers don't come out and buy the Jim Dandies."

"Oh," cried Betsy, "the Jim Dandies!"

"Sure," said Billy. "You see, I'm working for Jim and he's going to pay me, but not until I get a customer out. He's going to give me a chocolate Jim Dandy covered with nuts. They're much better covered with nuts, because the chocolate on the chocolate-covered ones is very thin. So you get more if you get one covered with nuts."

HONK! HONK! went the horn at the front gate.

"Hurry up, Betsy," said Billy. "Hurry up and get me a bell."

"But I don't know where there is a bell," said Betsy. She started to run toward the back door of the house. Billy and Star followed. "I have my ukulele." said Betsy. "Don't you think maybe I could help with my ukulele?"

"You sure you haven't got a bell?" asked Billy.

HONK! HONK! went the horn.

"There's a bell on the alarm clock," said Betsy. "What about the alarm clock? It has a very loud bell."

"No, you'd have to keep winding it up all the time," said Billy.

"What about a kazoo? I have a kazoo," Betsy suggested. "That makes a pretty loud noise."

HONK! HONK! from Jim.

"Well, bring it along," said Billy, starting for the door.

"Wait for me!" cried Star from her room. "Wait for me!"

Billy and Betsy hurried down the driveway toward the truck. "Now remember," Billy whispered, "if he asks you to go along, the chocolate with the nuts is the best."

"Well, did you get a bell?" Jim asked.

"Betsy's got a kazoo," said Billy. "Blow it, Betsy. Let Jim hear it."

Betsy blew into the kazoo. It screeched. "Very pretty," said Jim. "It sounds like the rats. Billy, you'd better stay here with your friend Betsy and make music."

Just then Star reached the truck. "Look!" she called out. Everyone looked. Star held up the triangle that she played in the kindergarten orchestra. She knocked it with her little rod. It sounded very much like the Jim Dandy bell before it was broken.

"Now that's more like it!" said Jim. "Star, go ask your mom if you can come with me. That will get the customers out."

"She can't go without me," said Betsy.

"Okay," said Jim. "Go ask your mother if you can both go."

Betsy ran back to the house. In a few minutes she came back with her mother. When Betsy's mother saw Jim she said, "Oh, it's you! Your mother told me you were driving the Jim Dandy truck this summer. Is there room enough for all of them?"

Jim grinned. "Yes," he said, "there's plenty of room."

"Will you get them back by five o'clock?" Betsy's mother asked.

"Yes, ma'am," Jim promised. "I'll take good care of them."

The three children climbed in beside Jim and they started off. Star insisted upon being the one to beat the triangle. Before they reached the corner a customer came out of one of the houses and bought five Jim Dandies. Billy's face fairly shone. "Some sale!" he said.

"Well, I guess you want your pay now," said Jim.

"What kind did you say you wanted?"

Billy, Betsy, and Star all sang out together, "Chocolate with nuts." Jim handed them each a Jim Dandy. Then they had to take turns eating and beating the triangle.

Business was very good the rest of the afternoon. Promptly at five o'clock Jim set Betsy and Star down in front of their house. Then he opened the back of the truck and took out three more Jim dandies. He handed one to each of the children. "Chocolate," he said, "with nuts."

4

Betsy's Property

Betsy was spending part of her summer vacation with an aunt and uncle who had a summer place along a rocky coast. The house was built on a seashore road just above the rocks. Sometimes Betsy woke up at night, and if she heard the waves dashing against the rocks she knew that it was high tide.

Betsy loved the rocks. She loved to take her lunch and a book and climb around until she found a smooth rock to settle down on. There was one big rock near the shoreline that she thought looked especially inviting, with the water lapping all around it.

One afternoon, Betsy decided to climb down to this special rock. Her aunt and uncle had gone over to visit with some friends who were staying at a nearby hotel. Susie, her aunt's collie, followed Betsy. Susie had already smelled the cookies that Betsy was carrying along with a library book.

When Betsy reached the big rock, she settled down and looked around her. She saw that there were many sailboats out that day. She had never been this far out on the rocks, and she was surprised to see how far away the houses on the road appeared. The cars on the road seemed much smaller, too. Betsy began to feel very much alone, but she wasn't afraid because she knew she could always climb over the rocks and reach the road again. After all, she had come down that way, so she could go back any time she wanted to.

Meanwhile, she had Susie, her cookies, and her book. Betsy felt that this big rock was her very own property. It was a place that belonged to her. Betsy liked the feeling of being rich and owning a part of the world. Since it was her very own, she could name it. She decided to call it Betsy's Point. There were all kinds of Points on this coast. There was Fisherman's Point, Green Point, and Seagull Point. Now there was Betsy's Point.

Betsy surveyed her property and was pleased with

what she saw. She liked to listen to the seagulls that flew around and dove into the water and came up with clams. She could hear the clam shells break as they fell from the seagulls' beaks onto the rocks.

Susie had settled down beside her, and Betsy felt very cozy. She took out her cookies and shared them with the dog. Then Betsy opened her book and began to read. She had borrowed the book from the local library. It was a book she had never read, and the very first page caught Betsy's interest, for she liked books about adventures. She read on and on, and she didn't notice that the sun had disappeared and that clouds were building up on the horizon. Another thing she didn't notice was that the water that had been lapping against the stone was now slapping the stone much harder than before.

Once, Betsy looked up. She looked out at the sea, and she saw that it was full of whitecaps. The wind was freshening. Once in a while she saw a sailboat, but there were not as many sailboats out now as there had been earlier in the afternoon.

Betsy went back to reading, and soon she was deep into the story of a man shipwrecked on what seemed to be a deserted island. Suddenly, Betsy heard the sound of thunder, and the spell of the desert island was quickly broken.

Betsy looked around, and she saw that her property appeared much smaller, and the water much nearer. The tide was coming in, and Betsy had learned enough about tides to know that the tide would bring water that could cover the rocks on the edge of the shore.

Betsy began to feel uneasy. What would she do if Betsy's Point became covered with the sea? Betsy stood up. She could see that it was growing darker and the thunder was louder. She began to feel frightened, knowing that a storm was not far away.

Waves were beginning to send spray over the rocks. Betsy realized that climbing back to the road would be much harder than coming down, and she probably would get wet. She cried out to the dog, "Oh, Susie! What should we do?"

Perhaps in sympathy, Susie barked, and Betsy patted her on the head. The space on the rock where she had been sitting had grown much smaller. Betsy picked up her book, for she couldn't let a library book get wet. Every once in a while a car passed on the road above, and Betsy waved to it, hoping the passengers would notice that she

✸ Summer Fun ✸

was stranded on the rock. But the people in the cars did not pay any attention to her. From time to time she shouted at a car, hoping that someone would hear her, but the strong wind that had come up carried her voice out to sea.

As each car approached, Betsy hoped that it would be her uncle and aunt returning. She wondered whether her aunt and uncle would know where she was.

Betsy looked at her watch and saw that it was almost five o'clock. Just as there was a terrific clap of thunder, Betsy saw her aunt and uncle drive up to the house and park the car.

"Susie, they're home! But you'll have to tell them where I am." Susie seemed to know that Betsy was in trouble, for she began to whine. "Go on, Susie," said Betsy. "Call them for me."

With this, Susie went into the water and swam to the nearest rocks on shore. Then she got up and shook herself and began to bark great, loud barks. Betsy called out, "That's right, Susie! That's right! Bark! Bark!"

Susie ran up the road and her barking became more and more alarming. Betsy's aunt and uncle came out on the porch, and they immediately saw that Betsy was stranded down on the big rock.

Betsy felt relieved when she saw her uncle cross the road and start climbing over the rocks. As he got closer to the water, with the waves dashing against the rocks, Betsy realized that her uncle was going to get very wet, and she knew that she, too, would get very wet.

Her uncle was coming nearer and nearer to where she was waiting. Finally she heard his voice. "I'm coming, Betsy," he called out. "Don't be afraid. I'll take care of you."

By this time the clouds had opened and the rain was pouring down. Betsy could feel it soaking her clothes, but she didn't care, she was so glad to see her uncle.

When her uncle finally gathered her into his arms, she didn't even care about the library book. She knew that she could pay for the book and the librarian would forgive her.

Now her uncle began his difficult climb back to the road. The rocks were very slippery and there were many times when he almost lost his footing. But Betsy held on tightly to her uncle and felt his strength as the surf blew against them.

When they finally reached the road Betsy heard

her uncle give a great big sigh of relief. Betsy, too, breathed more freely when at last, soaking wet, they reached the front door of the house where her aunt was waiting for them. Paying no attention to the condition of Betsy's clothes, her aunt threw her arms around her.

"Oh, dear Betsy!" she said. "I have been watching from the window while your uncle brought you over those rocks. And I am so grateful that you are both safely home."

Susie seemed to be glad to be home too, for she shook the water out of her coat and, with a sigh, lay down.

5.

Betsy's Hammock Club

Betsy's summer vacation was made especially happy when her father brought home a hammock that he hung between two apple trees. Betsy loved the hammock. If she pushed on the ground with her feet she could make it swing, but her delight was to lie in the hammock and read a book or snuggle up with her little sister, Star, and tell stories.

Before long all of the children in the neighborhood knew that Betsy had a hammock. Soon, almost every time Betsy went out of the house, she saw a child running away and the hammock swinging, and she knew that there had been a visitor in her hammock. Her invited friends, Ellen and Billy, came frequently for they, too, loved the hammock.

One day Betsy, from inside the house, heard Ellen and Billy quarreling. She ran out to them and said, "Are you fighting over the hammock again?"

"Well, it's my turn," said Billy. "Ellen's been in the hammock a long time and now it's my turn."

"I haven't been in it very long," said Ellen. "I had to chase a strange kid out of it. All the kids around here think this hammock is free."

"I know," said Betsy. "I don't know what I'm going to do about it."

"I know what we should do," said Billy.

"What?" said Betsy.

"We should form a club," said Billy. "Betsy, you can be the president."

"Thanks," said Betsy. "Of course I'll be president, 'cause it's my hammock."

"And Ellen and I will be the members. Charter members. Charter means that we get to use the hammock first whenever we want to," said Billy.

"But two people can't be first," said Ellen. "Only one person can be first."

"Well," said Betsy, "the very first is me 'cause I'm the president of the Hammock Club."

53

"Okay," said Billy. "But Ellen and I get the most chances to use the hammock after you, Betsy, 'cause we're the charter members. My father says charter members in clubs are very important so that makes Ellen and me very important. Now any kid who Betsy catches using her hammock must pay a fine, a dime, for stealing a ride in the hammock. How about that, Betsy? Is that all right?"

"Right," said Betsy.

One morning as Betsy's father left for his office he said to Betsy, "Betsy, darling, the garden needs watering. There is a sprinkler all set up in the center of the lawn and if you would turn it on at three o'clock this afternoon it will help the garden."

Betsy spent the morning lying in the hammock reading a book. After lunch she decided to color some pictures in a new coloring book. She sat at the dining room table with a box of crayons. When the bell on the hall clock struck three Betsy remembered that her father had told her to turn on the sprinkler to water the garden.

The sprinkler was the kind that sprayed water forward and then backward. Without looking around Betsy ran to the water spigot and turned it

on. In a moment the sprinkler sprayed water onto the garden.

Betsy had just entered the house when the sprinkler reversed and she heard something go bump, followed by a loud scream. Her mother, who was putting Betsy's sister, Star, down for a nap, called from upstairs, "Betsy, what's the matter?"

Betsy ran out of doors. The sprinkler was going back and forth, but to Betsy's great surprise she saw a girl lying on the ground. Her legs, covered with blue jeans, were flying around and the water from the sprinkler was falling on the hammock and the girl.

Betsy, paying no attention to the water, ran to the girl. She leaned down and said, "What are you doing here?"

"I fell out of the hammock," said the girl. "I was trying to get out of the rain. It must be raining very hard."

"It isn't raining," said Betsy. "It's the sprinkler watering the garden. But let me help you up. I'm getting very wet. Who are you and where do you come from?"

"I'm Polly," said the girl. "We just moved into a house down the street. You see, I was walking

by and I saw the hammock. It looked so nice I just had to lie down in it. All of a sudden it began to rain."

"As I said," said Betsy, "it's the water from the sprinkler. When I saw you with your legs flying around, I thought you were break dancing."

"I'm sorry," said Polly, "but you see I couldn't resist getting into the hammock. I was just taking a walk and hoping I would meet somebody to talk to."

"Well, you've met me," said Betsy. "My name is Betsy, and I'm sorry to tell you, but you'll have to give me a dime."

"I have to give you a dime," said Polly, "when I just fell out of your old hammock? And your old sprinkler has wet my hair and my clothes all over, and now you want me to give you a dime?"

"Well, you see," said Betsy, "my friends, Ellen and Billy, and I have a hammock club and I'm the president, and any kid who uses my hammock has to give me a dime."

"Well, I don't think it's fair," said Polly. "I didn't know you had a hammock club, so it isn't fair for you to ask me for a dime. Anyway, I don't have one."

"Well, I'm glad to meet you," said Betsy, "and you can forget the dime."

"Thanks," said Polly. "Hey, you're all wet, too."

Betsy laughed and said, "Yes, and I guess the hammock's soaked. But I suppose when I turn off the sprinkler we'll all dry off. My best friend, Ellen, will be here soon, and I guess Billy Porter will be over, too. They're the members of the club. They both love the hammock."

"Well, they won't be getting into it very soon," said Polly. "Not until it dries."

"When the sun comes out it will dry out, but not unless I turn off the sprinkler," said Betsy.

"Is Billy Porter your boyfriend?" Polly asked.

"Well, I don't call him my boyfriend," said Betsy. "I have a lot of friends who happen to be boys. Billy and I have been in the same class in school since first grade. Ellen's been in the same class with me, too. I guess you'll be in our class when we all go back in September. You'll like Ellen and Billy. We have a lot of fun together. Billy thought of the Hammock Club."

A few minutes later Ellen and Billy came running up the driveway. Neither Ellen nor Billy noticed the sprinkler, and before Betsy could cry out, the water was falling on Billy and Ellen. Betsy could see that they were both running toward the hammock, but they stopped short of it for they both saw that it was very wet.

Billy cried out, "What's going on?"

"I'm watering the garden," said Betsy.

"Well, you've watered me," said Billy.

"And me," said Ellen.

"And Polly here," said Betsy. "She's new here, and she's been waiting to meet you and Billy. She was in the hammock before she fell out and got wet."

"Did she give you a dime?" Billy asked.

"Oh, no," said Betsy, "because she fell out and got wet. I think we should ask her to join the club, 'cause I think she's going to be a new friend."

Polly smiled, and said, "Oh, I'd like to be a member of the Hammock Club and I hope we'll all be in the same class in school in September."

"Sure," said Billy, "and if Betsy will ever turn off the water, maybe the hammock will get dry, and tomorrow we'll all take turns in it."

Betsy ran and turned off the water.

When Betsy's father came home he said to Betsy, "Did you water the garden for me?"

"Oh, yes, Daddy," Betsy replied. "And I watered all my friends."

"Good," said her father, "that will make 'em grow."

· 6 ·

Eddie and His Hermit Crab

Anna Patricia Wallace and her parents had been at the seashore for two weeks. Anna Patricia's father, who was a dentist, had to come home to take care of some of his patients, but the Wallaces planned to return to the seashore later in the summer.

While she was at the seashore, Anna Patricia had become acquainted with hermit crabs. She had bought two of them from the man who had the hermit crab shop on the boardwalk. Now that she was back home, she had decided to give one of the crabs to her friend, Eddie Wilson.

Eddie had never seen hermit crabs before, and he was full of questions. "Why do they call them hermit crabs?" he asked his friend.

"Because they hide in the abandoned shells of other sea creatures," said Anna Patricia.

Eddie looked at his hermit crab carefully. "Such thin little legs," he said. "He couldn't stand up on those legs."

"Don't you worry about him," said Anna Patricia. "Just look at the way he climbs around in the cage."

"I guess I'll have to go out and buy him his own cage," said Eddie.

"You can keep him in an aquarium if you want to," said Anna Patricia, "but I think he can climb around better in a cage."

"Do they bite?" Eddie asked.

"They'll nip your little finger, but it doesn't hurt. That's the way you say good morning to them." Anna Patricia showed Eddie how the crab would nip her finger, and when Eddie did it, he thought it was great fun.

"Let's go buy a cage. I think I'd rather have him in a cage than in an aquarium."

Eddie ran to his mother and said, "Mom, I have to have some money to buy a cage for my crab."

"A cage for your crab!" his mother exclaimed.

"I've heard of bird cages, but I've never heard of crab cages."

"Well, you see, Mom, Annie Pat brought me a hermit crab. She brought it home from the seashore, and now she's giving it to me."

"Well," said his mother, "we've had a lot of pets around here, but this is something new." As she handed Eddie a five-dollar bill, she said, "Eddie, you are always full of surprises. I hope you won't spend all of the money. I never expected to have to buy a cage for a crab."

"Oh, I'm going to have a lot of fun with this little guy," said Eddie.

"You bet," said Anna Patricia. "The first of August they're going to have a hermit crab race down at the seashore, and my mother said that you could come down and visit us, and be there for the hermit crab race."

"You mean I could take my crab along, and he could be in the race?"

"That's right," said Anna Patricia. "We could each have a crab in the race."

The children went off to the pet shop, and when Eddie told the owner that he wanted a cage for his hermit crab, the man was just as surprised as Eddie's mother had been.

"Well, I've got all kinds of bird cages," he said, "but this is the first time somebody has wanted a crab cage. I guess you'll have to point it out."

"Just one made of chicken wire will do," said Anna Patricia.

"Well, if that's all you want," said the man, "I can make that up in a few minutes."

"Oh, that's great!" said Eddie. "I guess that won't cost very much."

"A couple of dollars," said the man. And sure enough, in a very short time, Eddie went off with his crab cage. The shopkeeper laughed as he watched the children go. "Crab cages," he chuckled to himself.

Before Anna Patricia left Eddie with the crab, she said, "Now, you have to feed the crab every two or three days. They like little bits of hamburger, pieces of cabbage, and apples. And don't forget to put a little dish of water in the cage."

"Gee!" said Eddie. "We've got a new member of the family. Do I have to cook the hamburger?"

"Oh, no," said Anna Patricia, laughing. "And

you don't have to put it on a bun, either!"

Eddie laughed. "I can't wait to get to the sea-shore and see that hermit crab race. I'll bet my crab will win."

"Oh, no," said Anna Patricia. "My crab's going to win the race."

"Well, we'll see," said Eddie. "I think my crab looks like a real athlete. I'm going to put him through training. I'll see that he gets plenty of ex-ercise."

When Anna Patricia said good-bye to Eddie that morning, she said, "Well, may the best crab win!"

"That's right," said Eddie. "I'm going to name my crab Punky."

"That's a good name," said Anna Patricia. "My crab's name is Lilly."

A few days before Eddie and Anna Patricia were to leave for the seashore with her parents, Anna Patricia went over to see how Eddie's hermit crab was.

"How's Punky?" Anna Patricia asked.

"Oh, Annie Pat!" exclaimed Eddie. "I don't think Punky feels very well. He hasn't been eating his hamburger, he hasn't been climbing around, and he doesn't nip my finger when I poke it into the cage."

Anna Patricia looked at the hermit crab. "Maybe his shell is too small. We should find a bigger one for him to move into. Maybe he's all cramped up in there. I've got a bigger shell than that at home," she said. "I'll run home and get it."

"Good idea," said Eddie. "It'll be moving day for Punky, and I hope it'll make him happy."

Anna Patricia was soon back with the shell. She and Eddie sat down, hoping to see Punky move into his new house. But Punky stayed put.

"He's just brooding," said Anna Patricia. "He'll probably move in in the middle of the night, and in the morning he'll be settled."

"I hope so," said Eddie. "I hope it will cheer him up."

The following morning, when Eddie looked in the cage, sure enough, Punky had moved into his new shell, and the old one was lying nearby. Eddie poked his finger into the cage and Punky nipped it, so Eddie felt that Punky was at least on the way to recovery. Later in the day he noticed that the crab had begun to eat his food again, and Eddie felt happier. Punky would be able to win the race after all!

At last the day came when Eddie went off with Anna Patricia and her parents to the seashore. Both of the children took their pet crabs along. Now that the children were settled at the seashore, they were looking forward to the hermit crab race.

On the day of the hermit crab race, Anna Patricia and Eddie were full of excitement. When they arrived at the beach, they were surprised to see how many children had gathered together with their hermit crabs. To Eddie's great delight, a photographer from the newspaper was there, as well as a TV camera crew.

The children crowded around a low table that had been placed in the shade under the boardwalk. The man who sold hermit crabs was in charge. The children watched with great interest as they saw him place all of the crabs in the center of the table. There was a great deal of wiggling and crawling, but finally he had them all gathered together.

Eddie kept his eye on Punky, and he kept saying to himself, "Now, go for it, Punky! As soon as he blows the whistle, go for it!"

The children saw the crab man put a plastic cake cover over the bunch of hermit crabs in the center of the table.

"Now," said the man, "as soon as I remove this cover, the crabs will scramble hither and thither, and the first one that falls off the table onto the sand will be considered the winner."

Now the cover was removed, and there was a great shout from all of the children as they watched their crabs crawl in all directions, each child hoping that his crab would be the first one to fall off the table.

"Go for it, go for it, go for it!" the children shouted at their crabs. Then, suddenly, Eddie's voice rose above the others.

"There goes Punky, off the table! He won! He won!" Eddie knelt down in the sand and picked up his hermit crab. "Good boy," he said. "Good boy! You're a gold-medal winner!"

When Eddie stood up, he was surprised that the crab man really handed him a small gold medal.

"Congratulations!" said the man. "Eddie Wilson's hermit crab has won the race."

✳ Eddie and His Hermit Crab ✳

And even the children who were disappointed clapped for Punky.

Eddie's photograph was taken with his hermit crab, and when the photographer asked him for his name and address he said, "Will I see myself in the newspaper?"

"You sure will," said the photographer.

Eddie called out to Anna Patricia, "Did you hear that, Annie Pat? Punky and I are going to be in the newspaper!"

Anna Patricia laughed and said, "Oh, Eddie. That makes you a famous person. And you're the first famous person I ever knew."

Eddie held up his crab and said, "I guess it's Punky that's famous."

That evening when the news came on TV, there was Eddie with his crab. And Eddie really felt like an important person.

"Oh, Eddie, do you think I'll ever see myself on TV?" said Anna Patricia.

"Sure you will, Annie Pat," said Eddie. "Some day you'll be Miss America."

Eddie and His Money Sheet

Eddie Wilson was enjoying his visit with Anna Patricia at the seashore cottage that her father had rented.

Eddie had brought his bicycle with him and he found it great fun to ride it on the boardwalk. The boards were laid so that bicycles could wheel along smoothly.

One morning when Eddie was riding on the boardwalk he came to a group of people who were gathered together by the railing. They were all looking down at something on the sand. Of course, Eddie got off of his bicycle and joined the crowd. He leaned over and looked down. He was surprised to see, made out of sand, the head of an Indian wearing a feather headdress.

Eddie heard someone in the crowd say, "Hey, that guy's a good sculptor." And somebody replied, "Sure is, and it's all made out of wet sand instead of clay."

Then Eddie saw a man walking toward them carrying a bucket of water. The man put the bucket down and picked up some sand. Eddie watched with great interest to see what the man was going to do with the wet sand, for there was already something in the sand that looked like the muzzle of a horse.

Eddie noticed that there was a sheet laid out beside the sculpture on which there were several coins. Painted on the sheet was the word "thanks," so Eddie realized that the artist was collecting money from the spectators.

"Oh, boy," said Eddie to himself, "this is great. I could do this and make some money."

Eddie got on his bicycle and started back to the cottage. When he went in the front door he met Anna Patricia's mother.

"Oh, Mrs. Wallace," he said, "do you have a piece of old sheet that I could have?"

"An old sheet?" said Mrs. Wallace. "What do you want with an old sheet?"

"Oh, I just got an idea," said Eddie. "I'm going to make some money."

"You're going to make some money with an old sheet?" said Anna Patricia's mother.

Anna Patricia, who had just come into the room, said, "Oh, Mom, Eddie can make money out of anything."

"Well, if he can make it out of an old sheet he's a real financier," said her mother.

"Have you got one?" Eddie asked, rather impatiently.

"As a matter of fact," said Mrs. Wallace, "I took an old one off of one of the beds this morning. It's the last thing I put in the laundry hamper. Eddie, you can tear off as much as you want from that sheet. I don't have time because I'm going to do the shopping."

Soon Eddie, dragging the sheet, returned to Anna Patricia. "Hey, Annie Pat," he said, "when I opened the laundry hamper your cat jumped out of it."

"Oh, Eddie," exclaimed Anna Patricia, "how could our cat have jumped out of the laundry hamper when we don't even have a cat!"

"Well, he did," said Eddie, "and I just opened

the screen door for him so he could get out."

"Well, how did he get in?" said Anna Patricia.

"I don't know," said Eddie, "but maybe he's the cat that I let in this morning. There was a cat scratching at the screen door so I let him in. I thought he was your cat."

"But, Eddie," said Anna Patricia, "how could he be our cat when we don't have a cat?"

"Well, I don't know about your cat," said Eddie. "I just know a cat jumped out of the laundry hamper and that cat is scratching at the screen door right now. Maybe he thinks he's your cat."

"Well, he can stop thinking it," said Anna Patricia, "because, as I just told you, we don't have a cat."

"I get you," said Eddie. "But maybe this cat is looking for a home. Wouldn't you like to have a nice cat?"

"I don't like cats," said Anna Patricia. "Anyway, not very much."

"But this looks like such a nice cat," said Eddie. "He's a yellow cat with dark stripes on his back."

"I don't like yellow cats," said Anna Patricia.

"Well, he's not all yellow," said Eddie. "I told

you he has dark stripes on his back. And he has beautiful eyes."

"Oh, Eddie," said Anna Patricia, "how could you see his eyes when he was all shut up in the clothes hamper?"

"Didn't I let him in?" said Eddie. "And didn't I let him out? All the time I thought it was your cat."

"You don't seem to understand, Eddie. I told you before, we don't have a cat."

"You sure you don't want him?" said Eddie.

"I told you, Eddie, I don't like yellow cats."

"But this one has dark stripes on his back. He hardly looks yellow at all," said Eddie. "And when he runs fast you hardly notice the yellow at all. I think he's a tiger cat. He has a little black nose, too. He's very cute."

"You mean he really does have dark stripes," said Anna Patricia, "and a black nose?"

"That's right," said Eddie. "You'd hardly notice the yellow at all."

"Oh, Eddie," cried Anna Patricia, "do you really think he's a tiger cat?"

"Oh, I guess that's what he is," said Eddie, "a tiger cat."

"Oh," exclaimed Anna Patricia, "I just love tiger cats. Is he still scratching on the screen door?"

"That's right," said Eddie.

"Well, don't let him scratch on the screen door," said Anna Patricia. "Go let him in."

Eddie went to the screen door, and as he opened it, he said, "Come on in, Buster, you got yourself a home."

When Anna Patricia saw the cat she exclaimed, "Oh, you sweet pussycat, did that naughty boy tell you that I didn't like cats? It's just catty cats that I don't like. But tiger cats are different. You can live right here with me."

It wasn't long before Anna Patricia's mother came home. She found the cat prowling around the living room. "Anna Patricia," she cried, "where did this cat come from?"

"Why, he's our cat," said Anna Patricia.

"Our cat?" said her mother. "We don't have a cat."

"Oh, yes," said Eddie, "you have a cat now. Annie Pat just adopted him, and I named him Buster and I let him in."

"Well, you can let him out," said Mrs. Wallace.

"Oh, no," said Anna Patricia, "you see, I adopted him. And when you adopt something it's forever."

"Oh, dear," said her mother. "Well, you can't adopt this cat until you find out whom he belongs to." Then she added, "Eddie, when I left you, you were about to make money out of a torn sheet. What happened to your big business project?"

"Oh, yes," said Eddie. "You see, Mrs. Wallace, when I went to the clothes hamper this cat jumped out."

"Don't tell me any more," said Anna Patricia's mother. "Get on with your big business. How much of a sheet do you want?"

Eddie looked at the sheet and said, "I guess half of it would be enough. I guess I won't catch much money the first day."

"Catch money?" exclaimed Anna Patricia. "Eddie, you do have the craziest ideas!"

"Well," said Eddie, "I'm very good at finding homes for cats."

Then Eddie picked up his piece of sheet, folded it, and put it under his arm. As he went out the door, he called back, "I'll see you later when I bring back all my money."

"Sorry I can't go with you, Eddie," Anna Patricia called out, "but I have to go with my mother to get new shoes."

Outside he picked up his tin bucket and shovel and started for the beach. He noticed that there were four big clam shells in the bucket. "They might be useful," he thought.

Eddie had to hold tightly to the sheet, for there was a strong sea breeze blowing. He hadn't gone far when he lost his grip on the sheet and the strong breeze blew it open and wrapped it around Eddie.

As a teenage boy on a bicycle passed Eddie, he yelled, "Happy Halloween, Ghostie!"

Struggling with the sheet with his one free hand, Eddie pressed on to the beach. He walked under the boardwalk and selected a place for his sand sculpture. He put down his sheet and fastened the four corners down with the large clam shells that were in his bucket. Then he ran to the edge of the ocean and filled his bucket with water. Soon he was at work with damp sand, modeling a cat, of course, for cats were on Eddie's mind.

When he finished it he thought it was what Anna Patricia would call a real "catty cat."

Eddie had placed his sheet close to a ramp that

Eddie and His Money Sheet

led from the boardwalk down to the sand. Soon a young man and a woman came down the ramp. They stopped and looked at Eddie's work.

"Oh, look!" said the girl. "Look at the monkey that kid made."

"It's a cat," said Eddie.

"Sure it's a cat," said the man, and he threw a nickel onto Eddie's sheet.

Later a man came running down the ramp and without stopping threw a nickel onto Eddie's sheet.

Eddie called back to the man, "Thanks."

Eddie was busy modeling a racing car when a policeman came up to him and said, "Let me see your license."

"License?" said Eddie.

"That's right," said the policeman. "You can't carry on a business in this town without a license."

"Well, I've only made ten cents," said Eddie, holding out the money. "Here, you can have it."

The policeman shook his head. "Oh, no," he said, "I'm an officer of the law. You can't buy police protection from me."

Eddie looked worried. "You mean I'm going to be arrested?" he asked.

"Well," said the policeman, "as long as it's your first offense against the law I won't turn you in."

"Oh, thanks," said Eddie. "But I can't go back to the house without any money. I came out to make some money."

"I'll tell you what to do," said the policeman. "You take your bucket and go on down the beach to that sand sculptor. Maybe he'll pay you for carrying buckets of water for him."

Eddie grabbed up his bucket and ran down the beach to where the sand sculptor was working.

"Hey, Mister," said Eddie, "do you need somebody to carry buckets of water for you? I'll do it for a nickel a bucket."

The man looked down at Eddie and said, "Okay, kid, but that's expensive water. How about three cents a bucket?"

"Okay," said Eddie.

By the end of the morning Eddie had made thirty cents. As he left the beach he looked out over the ocean. At first he thought he saw a sailboat, but then he realized that what he was seeing was his money sheet flying out over the ocean.

When Eddie got back to the house he found Anna Patricia admiring her new shoes.

"Hello, Eddie," she said. "What about all that money you were going to make? How much did you earn?"

Eddie held out his thirty cents and said, "I made thirty cents."

"Thirty cents?" said Anna Patricia. "Why, that won't even buy a hot dog!"

"Well, I don't want a hot dog," said Eddie. "It would spoil my lunch."

Anna Patricia began to giggle, and Eddie knew that Anna Patricia's giggles were worth paying attention to.

"So what, Annie Pat?" said Eddie.

Anna Patricia giggled some more. "Isn't it funny, Eddie," she said, "that nobody ever thought of making hot cats."

Eddie roared with laughter. "Hot cats!" he cried. "That would be something!"

·8·

The Picnic

Anna Patricia and Eddie were sitting on the front steps of the porch. They were watching a little boy who was coming up the street apparently looking for something. Eddie said to Anna Patricia, "Bet he's looking for a tiger cat."

"Oh, no," said Anna Patricia. "I don't want to part with that cat. I love that cat! I hope he isn't looking for a cat."

"Well, we'll soon know," said Eddie.

The little boy came toward them, and when he reached the house next door he ran up the steps and looked all around the porch. Then he came down, and he came over to them and said, "Have you seen my cat?"

"Oh," said Anna Patricia. "What kind of a cat is it?"

"He's a tiger cat," said the boy. "You see, we used to live in this house next door, but now we live over on the bay. I thought maybe Snickers had come back thinking that he lived here. You know, animals do that sometimes. Sometimes they walk miles trying to find their way back to where they were before. I thought maybe Snickers had done that, and that he was back here."

"Wait just a minute," said Anna Patricia. "I think I have your cat."

Anna Patricia went inside the house and in a few moments she brought out the cat and handed him to the little boy.

He took him in his arms and he fondled him, and he said, "Oh, Snickers! Why did you run away? I've been looking all over for you. I'm so glad to see you again. I've missed you so much!"

Anna Patricia looked very sad. "I was hoping I could keep your cat," she told the boy.

"Well, you can come and visit him anytime," said the boy. "My name's Jake, and as I said, we live over on the bay. Do you ever go over to the bay?"

"Sometimes we go over on our bikes," said Eddie. "We go to look at the marina with all the boats. Those sailboats are neat."

"Yes, they are," said the boy. "Do you have a sailboat?"

"Oh, no, we don't have a sailboat," said Anna Patricia. "Do you?"

"Oh, we have two sailboats," said Jake. "My father has a sloop. It has two sails. And my brother, Andy, has a catboat. It just has one sail, but it's a swell boat. Why don't you come over sometime? My brother will take you for a sail. You could find our house easily. Our name is Butler. Remember—it's not Butter, it's Butler. But you can remember it by remembering Butter. It's a good way to remember our name, Butler. There's a big sign outside of our place. It has my father's name on it, so you wouldn't have any trouble finding it. Come over sometime."

"Oh, that would be great," said Eddie. "I love sailboats."

"Well, I've never been in a sailboat," said Anna Patricia, "but I guess I would like it very much. We'll come over sometime."

Jake waved to the children and said, "Thanks a lot for taking care of Snickers," and he went off with his cat.

Anna Patricia and Eddie lost no time in going over to the bay. In the afternoon they got on their bicycles and they biked over to the bay area. They admired the boats again, and they looked around for the sign that said Butler. It didn't take long to find it. They also found Jake and another boy on the dock, right in front of the house that had the sign BUTLER on it.

When Jake saw the children he waved and said, "Hi! You came over, didn't you? This is my brother Andy."

Anna Patricia and Eddie said, "Hi, Andy."

Andy said, "Hi. I hear you would like to go for a sail."

"Oh, yes, we would," said Eddie.

"Look," said Andy, "tomorrow's Saturday, and we're going to have a picnic. We like to go across the bay to a house that belongs to a friend of my father's. They're away now, but we can go over there and have a picnic. They have a big outdoor grill. So why don't you come over? Come about half-past eleven and join us for the picnic."

"That would be great!" said Anna Patricia and Eddie in a chorus.

"We'll be here for sure," said Eddie. "I love going out in a sailboat."

Eddie and Anna Patricia hung around a while, admiring the sailboats in the marina, and Andy's and his father's boats. They were not in the marina. Mr. Butler's sailboat was right by the dock, but Andy's was moored about thirty feet from the dock. Eddie pointed to it and said, "How do you get out to your sailboat?"

"Oh, we use this rowboat that you see here, and we row out to the sailboat and climb in."

Later in the afternoon Anna Patricia and Eddie got on their bicycles and went back home. They could hardly wait for the next day to come, they were both so anxious to go out on that sailboat and to have a picnic with Andy and Jake. It was going to be a wonderful day.

The following morning Anna Patricia and Eddie woke up early. Their minds were on the sailboat and the picnic. The children put their bathing suits on first thing in the morning. They kept looking at the clock and didn't want to be late.

At eleven o'clock they were both on their bicycles, taking off for the bay. Again they saw Jake and Andy on the dock, but they didn't see any picnic basket. However, they parked their bicycles and went down to the dock, and said hi to the boys.

"Good to see you!" said Andy.

"Hi," said Jake.

"Where's the picnic lunch?" Anna Patricia asked.

"Our father and mother are going to bring the picnic basket over in my father's sailboat," Andy said. "My mother's fixing the lunch now. I'm going to take you three over, and we'll wait for them over there. Are you ready to go?"

"Yes!" cried Eddie and Anna Patricia.

"Good," said Andy. "You two get into the rowboat. Then Jake and I will get in, and we'll row out to the sailboat. Our life jackets are in the rowboat. Be sure to put one on."

When the children were all in the rowboat, Andy said to Eddie, "Would you like to row?"

"Sure!" said Eddie. He picked up the oars and began to use them. But instead of going toward the sailboat, the rowboat began to go around and around and around.

"Don't you know how to row?" said Andy.

"Oh, I'll get the hang of it in a minute," said Eddie. And with that, one of the oars slipped out of his hand and floated off in the water.

"Oh!" said Andy. "You've lost an oar! You'll never be able to get over. I'll go get it."

Andy jumped into the water and swam out to where the oar was floating, and brought it back to Eddie.

Eddie got it securely fastened in the oarlock, and Andy showed him how to pull the oars. This time Eddie was able to get the rowboat to go toward the sailboat.

When they reached the sailboat, Andy climbed in, and then he reached out his hand to help Anna Patricia. But Anna Patricia, instead of getting into the sailboat, fell into the water.

"Oh, no!" said Andy. "You missed it! Now you have to try again. Good thing you've got your life jacket on."

Anna Patricia splashed around for a minute and then she took hold of Andy's hand again, and this time she made it into the sailboat.

Eddie and Jake didn't have any difficulty getting into the sailboat. Then Andy fastened the rowboat to the end of the sailboat so that it

✴ Summer Fun ✴

wouldn't get away from them. There was a nice breeze blowing, and it caught the sail, and in a very short time they were in the middle of the bay.

"Well, how do you like being in a sailboat, Annie Pat?" Eddie asked.

"Oh, it's wonderful!" said Anna Patricia, "but why do they call it a kittyboat?"

"It isn't a kittyboat, Annie Pat," said Eddie. "It's a catboat."

"Why do they call it a catboat?" asked Anna Patricia. "Why don't they call it a dogboat?"

"I guess," said Andy, "for the same reason they don't call it a bunnyboat."

"Well, I think it's wonderful," said Anna Patricia. "It reminds me of coasting downhill on my bicycle, only better."

"You mean wetter!" said Eddie, and the children laughed.

Soon the sailboat reached the other side of the bay. Andy got the sailboat to the wharf and fastened it securely. Then he helped Anna Patricia out. The boys all climbed out very quickly.

Andy led the way to the house where they were

to have the picnic. As they went up the steps to the porch, Anna Patricia said, "Oh, boy! Am I hungry!"

"That's too bad," said Andy, "because we won't have any food until my father and mother bring the picnic basket over."

"I hope they come soon," said Anna Patricia, "because I'm hungry. Do you suppose there's a bag of pretzels in that house?"

"Well, we don't have any way to get in," said Jake. "My father has the keys to the house."

"Well, if Goldilocks was able to get into the bears' house, I'll bet I can get into this one," said Anna Patricia. And she went over to one of the windows and tried to push it open.

She pushed and she pushed, and suddenly the window flew up and the burglar alarm went off! It made a terrific racket!

"Well, Goldipat," said Eddie, "now you did it!"

"Oh, boy!" said Andy. "We'll have the police here now in no time at all. They'll come in the police launch. You see if I'm not right."

Sure enough, in just a few minutes, the police launch arrived and two policemen came up on the porch.

"Well," said one of the policemen. "What do you think you're doing? Are you trying to break into this house to rob it? You're a fine set of robbers!"

"It was Goldilocks here," said Jake. "She opened the window, and it set off the alarm."

"It certainly did," said the policeman. "I wonder who around here has the key that can shut it off, because we have to turn it off. It can't go all day."

"Well, my father has the key," said Andy.

"And where is your father?" asked the policeman.

"He and my mother are sailing over to meet us. They should be coming soon," said Andy.

Andy and Jake ran down to the dock, followed by Eddie, Anna Patricia, and the two policemen. They looked out across the bay. There, in the Butlers' sailboat, were the boys' parents. They waved at the children, and everyone waved back. But their boat was not moving. It was sitting perfectly still, and so were the other sailboats on the bay.

"They're becalmed!" Andy cried. "And if they're becalmed, they won't get over here until one o'clock, because that south wind won't be up be-fore one o'clock."

"Oh, no!" the children cried.

"Well, maybe he can't get over here, but we can get over to him," said the policeman. "And that's just exactly what I'm going to do, because I have to get the key to turn off this alarm."

The children watched the two policemen get into their motorboat and set off to get the key to shut off the alarm. They watched them as they approached Mr. Butler's sailboat, and they saw one of the policemen talk to Mr. Butler, and then he took something from Mr. Butler's hand.

The next thing the children saw made them yell for joy, for they saw Mrs. Butler hand the picnic basket over to the policemen, and they saw the policemen put it into the launch. It wasn't long before the policemen in the launch came back to the children. One handed the picnic basket to Andy, and the other ran up the steps and turned off the alarm.

It was a great relief to get rid of that terrible noise. People on nearby docks waved, and yelled, "Thanks! Thanks!"

Andy looked at his watch and said, "It won't

be long now before it'll be one o'clock. The south breeze will come up and they'll be over here before long. Meanwhile, we can each have a sandwich."

"Good!" said Anna Patricia. "That's even better than a pretzel."

Soon the children were sitting on the dock, dangling their feet in the water and eating sandwiches. Jake pointed to the picnic basket and said, "You know what's in that basket?"

"What?" said Anna Patricia.

"Hot dogs!" said Jake.

"Hot dogs—what about hot cats?" said Anna Patricia.

The boys all laughed. "Who ever heard of hot cats?" said Jake.

"Well, I guess nobody but Annie Pat," said Eddie. "She's always coming up with new ideas."

"Well," said Anna Patricia, "maybe when I grow up I'll introduce hot cats to the world, and I'll make a million dollars."

At last, as the children watched, a breeze came up, and sailboats all over the bay began to move. Mr. Butler brought his sailboat over to the children.

As Mr. Butler helped the boys' mother out of the sailboat he said, "That was some racket you kids made!"

"It was Annie Pat," said Eddie. "She thought she could get a pretzel. Annie Pat always thinks she can do something that nobody else can do."

"Well," said Anna Patricia, "Goldilocks did it."

"Yes," said Eddie, "Goldilocks did it, but the bears didn't have a burglar alarm! That's the difference."

"Well," said Mr. Butler, "now we can have a real picnic. I'll open up that basket and get out the hot dogs."

Under her breath, Anna Patricia said, "Hot cats."

"Dad," said Jake, "Goldipat has a wonderful idea. When she grows up she's going to make hot cats, and she's going to make a million dollars."

"Good for her!" said Mr. Butler. "I hope I can join her company."

❋ 9 ❋

An Afternoon on the Farm

Teddy and Babs Robinson were brother and sister. Teddy was six years old, and Babs was four. They lived in a tall apartment house in a big city, but now it was their daddy's vacation time, and Teddy and Babs were staying with their parents on a farm that belonged to Mr. and Mrs. Perkins.

Teddy had thought the farm might be very lonely. But when they arrived, he found to his delight that the Perkinses' grandchildren were staying with Mr. and Mrs. Perkins. The grandchildren were twins, Mark and Sarah. They had just had their seventh birthday.

The twins had two puppies. They were corgies, and the children loved them. Their names were Jack and Jill.

The children played together, and Mark and Sarah introduced Teddy and Babs to all of the animals on the farm: to the horses, to the cows, and even to the pigs.

It wasn't long before the Robinson children felt very much at home with all of the animals on the farm, and Teddy and Babs had become close friends with the twins. They did everything together.

One day, the four children lay in the tall grass in the nearby meadow. It was a warm, sunny afternoon. Sarah was watching the white, fleecy clouds chase each other across the blue sky. Teddy was looking at an ant that was climbing up a blade of grass. Jack and Jill lay curled up in balls. They were enjoying an afternoon nap.

"Let's do something," said Mark.

"What shall we do?" asked Sarah.

"We could pick blueberries," said Babs.

"Aw, I'm tired of picking blueberries," said Teddy. "Every time we go out, you want to pick blueberries."

"Let's play explorers," said Mark.

"What's 'splorers?" asked Babs.

"Explorers are people that go out and find things," said Mark. "Like Christopher Columbus.

He went out in a big ship and found America."

"Well, what will we find?" Teddy asked.

"Oh, you don't know what you're going to find," said Mark. "It's always a surprise."

"Like Christopher Columbus?" asked Babs.

"Sure," said Mark, "like Christopher Columbus. He was surprised when he found America."

"Where shall we go to explore?" asked Sarah.

"Let's go up the hill to the woods," said Mark. "We can make believe it's a new country and that we have never been there before."

"I thought we were going in a boat," said Babs. "Like Christopher Columbus."

"Oh, you don't have to go in a boat," said Mark. "You can explore on the land. You just walk until you discover something you never saw before."

"All right," said Teddy. "Let's be explorers."

The children started up the hill. They walked one behind the other. Jack and Jill ran ahead, sniffing here and there.

When the children reached the woods, Teddy said, "You know, we should have guns. Explorers always have guns."

"Why?" asked Babs.

"Because they might meet wild animals," replied Mark. "Explorers always bring home bears and things."

"Did Christopher Columbus bring home bears?" asked Babs.

"No," replied Mark, "he brought home wampum."

Teddy picked up a long stick. "This is my gun," he said. "I'll shoot any old bear that comes along."

After a while Sarah found a long stick. "I have a gun, too," she said, putting it over her shoulder.

"You wouldn't shoot a baby bear, would you?" asked Babs.

"No, just big grizzlies," replied Teddy.

"We could take one home and use the skin for a rug," said Sarah.

Soon Mark and Babs found sticks that they could use for guns. The four children tramped on through the woods.

"Do you think we will find anything?" asked Babs.

" 'Course we'll find something," said Mark. "Explorers always find something."

Just then, Jack and Jill stopped still. They lifted their heads and sniffed. Their noses twitched.

"Sniff! Sniff! Sniff!" Then their noses went down to the ground. "Sniff! Sniff! Sniff!" Like a flash they were off. The children left the path to follow the dogs. In a few moments the dogs began to bark. Mark ran ahead. When he reached the dogs, he found them standing over a little animal. The animal lay beside an old tree stump.

"Oh, look!" cried Mark, as the other children approached. "Look at the little animal. Somebody must have shot it with a real gun."

Jack began to shake the animal.

"Drop it, Jack!" said Mark. "Leave it alone."

Jack dropped it. The children stooped down to examine the animal.

"What do you suppose it is?" asked Sarah.

"Maybe it's a baby bear," said Babs.

"No," replied Mark, "it isn't a baby bear. Bears don't have white stripes on their backs."

"It has a pretty skin," said Teddy, stroking the fur.

"It smells funny," said Sarah.

"I don't smell anything," said Mark.

"Let's take it home," said Teddy.

"Yes," said Mark. "Maybe Grandaddy could skin it for us."

"It would make my doll a fur coat," said Sarah.

"Do you think I could have the tail for my bi-cycle?" asked Mark.

"I guess so," said Teddy. "It was your dog who found it."

"Well, let's take it home anyway," said Sarah. "We're explorers, and we can make believe we're bringing home a bear."

"Can I carry it?" asked Babs.

Mark picked up the animal and placed it in Babs' arms.

"I think it's terrible to shoot little animals," said Babs, almost in tears.

The children started for home. They had gone far into the woods so that it was a long way back. Soon Babs grew tired of carrying the little animal. "Here, Sarah," she said, "you carry it a while."

Sarah took the animal. "I think it smells sort of funny," she said.

"Girls are so fussy," said Mark. "Always think-ing about how things smell."

"Well, then, you carry it," said Sarah, handing it to Mark.

Mark carried the animal a long way. Finally

Teddy said, "I'd like to carry it a little while, Mark."

"All right," said Mark.

When the children reached home, Teddy was carrying the little animal close against his chest. As they neared the house they could see Mr. Perkins mowing the grass by the driveway.

"Oh, Grandaddy," cried Mark, "look what we found in the woods."

"We've been 'sploring!" shouted Babs.

"We've brought home a bear," cried Teddy.

Mr. Perkins left his lawnmower and came toward the children. "Gracious! Goodness!" he cried. "What have you brought home?"

Teddy held up the animal.

"Oh, my stars and buttons!" shouted Mr. Perkins. "It's a skunk! Can't you smell it? Oh, my goodness! Whatever made you bring home a skunk?"

"It's pretty, Grandaddy," said Mark. "We thought that you could skin it for us."

"Jumping junipers!" cried Mr. Perkins. "Put it in this basket and don't go in the house. You could smell the four of you in seven states! Sit right down

103

on this bench until I come back."

Teddy dropped the skunk into an old basket. Then the children sat down in a row on the bench. They were so surprised they couldn't think of any-thing to say, so they just sat still, swinging their legs.

Mr. Perkins went into the house. When he re-turned, Mrs. Perkins was with him. "Land sakes!" cried Mrs. Perkins. "I never smelled anything so awful. We'll have to burn their clothes and give them baths before they can go into the house."

Mr. Perkins brought out an old wooden wash-tub and placed it under the outdoor faucet at the back of the house. When the tub was full of water, Mrs. Perkins said, "Come now, you two boys, take off your clothes and get into this tub."

"You mean we have to take off our clothes out here?" said Mark.

"Yes! Every stitch," said Mrs. Perkins.

Teddy and Mark took their clothes off, and Mr. Perkins picked the clothes up with the end of a pole and dropped them in a wire basket.

"Now, get in the tub," said Mrs. Perkins.

Mark and Teddy stepped into the tub, and Mrs. Perkins began scrubbing them with a brush and

✸ An Afternoon on the Farm ✸

some soap. She scrubbed them all over. Then she washed their hair.

Sarah and Babs sat on the bench waiting for their turn.

When Mrs. Perkins was through with the boys, she gave them each a towel. Mark and Teddy ran indoors.

"Come along now," Mrs. Perkins called to the two little girls.

The girls took off their clothes while Mrs. Perkins filled up the tub a second time. Again Mr. Perkins picked up the little pile of clothes with the end of a pole. When he had dropped them into the basket, he put a match to the clothes. In a few minutes there were just a few ashes.

Sarah and Babs stepped into the tub, and Mrs. Perkins set to work again with her brush and soap. She washed their hair and rinsed it under the faucet. Then she gave them each a towel and sent them scampering.

When Babs ran through the kitchen door, her mother threw up her hands. "Sakes alive!" she cried. "First the two boys come running in without a stitch on, and now here come the girls. What did you do with your clothes?"

"Mr. Perkins burned them," said Babs, as she tramped up the back stairs.

Outside, Mrs. Perkins emptied the tub. "Well, that's over," she said.

Just then Jack and Jill appeared. They ran to Mrs. Perkins.

"Phew!" said Mrs. Perkins. "I declare, you smell worse than the children."

Once more she filled the tub. Then she picked up Jack and Jill and put them in the water. She scrubbed the little dogs, just as she had scrubbed the children. At last she lifted them out of the water. The dogs shook themselves very hard. Then they ran up and down the lawn and rolled on the newly cut grass.

Meanwhile, Mr. Perkins dug a deep hole and buried the skunk.

After dinner, the four children were sitting on the porch step. They looked like shiny new pennies in their clean clothes. Sarah's hair was still damp.

"What did your grandaddy say that little animal was?" asked Babs.

"It was a skunk," said Mark.

"I told you it smelled funny," said Sarah.

"I guess it did," said Mark.

"Well, we went exploring," said Teddy. "And we brought something home with us."

"Yes," said Babs, "just like Christopher Columbus. Only he brought wampum."

End of Summer

The days were growing shorter, and the leaves on the trees were beginning to turn red and yellow. Teddy and Babs and the twins, Mark and Sarah, no longer played out of doors after dinner. They gathered in front of the open fire and popped corn and toasted marshmallows. Every day they could see great flocks of birds flying toward the south.

One day Mark said, "Pretty soon Sarah and I will be going south. We have to go back to school soon. Wouldn't it be fun if we could just ride on one of those birds instead of going in the train? I'll bet they fly right over our house near Washington."

"I think it's fun to go on those old trains," said Sarah. "I like to listen to the engine. It always says,

'Got chur baggage! Got chur baggage! Got chur baggage!' "

"Is it very far to where you live?" asked Teddy.

"It's pretty far," said Mark.

"We have to take our lunch with us," said Sarah. "Grandmother always gives us a good lunch to eat on the train."

"Do you go all by yourselves?" asked Babs.

"Yes," replied Sarah, "all by ourselves."

"Oh, Grandaddy puts us on the train and he tells the conductor to take care of us. Then the conductor puts us off at Washington, and our daddy is always there to meet us."

"That must be fun," said Teddy. "I would like that."

"Well, it won't be long now before we'll go," said Sarah.

When the day arrived for the twins to leave, there was a great deal of excitement. Grandmother had packed their bags the day before and Grandaddy had taken them to the station in the station wagon. Now Mark and Sarah kept finding things that they wanted to take home with them.

"Oh, Grandmother!" cried Sara. "Here's my doll,

Hannah, and all of her clothes. What shall I do with her?"

"Dear, dear!" said Grandmother. "Hannah and her clothes should have gone in the suitcase. Now you will have to carry her."

"Grandmother!" Mark called. "I have to take my air gun and my new fishing rod. Daddy might take me fishing some day."

"Well, Grandaddy will have to wrap them up for you," said Grandmother.

Just then Sarah came running into the kitchen. "Grandmother! Grandmother!" she panted. "What do you think Mary up the road gave me for a going-away present?"

"I can't imagine," said Grandmother.

"She gave me her canary. The cage and everything."

"Well, I don't see how you'll be able to go on the train with a bird cage," said Grandmother.

"Oh, I can carry it," said Sarah.

Grandmother was busy making sandwiches. She packed the twins' lunch in a big square box. There were three kinds of sandwiches, cookies, and hard-boiled eggs. There were plums and two big, round peppermint patties. There was a big banana for each of them and some peanut-butter crackers.

"Now, do be careful, when you eat your lunch, not to drop papers on the floor. Let the people on the train see that you know how to mind your manners," said Grandmother.

The children promised to be very careful.

After awhile, Mark burst into the kitchen. "Look, Grandmother!" he cried. Grandaddy says I can take Barney home with me. He says he's mine to keep." Mark was carrying a great big turtle.

"Now, you can't take a turtle on the train with you," said Grandmother.

"Why not, Grandmother? He wouldn't be any trouble," said Mark. "I can get Grandaddy to put him in a box with holes punched in the lid."

"Well, go talk to him about it."

Mark rushed out, carrying the turtle.

When it was time to leave for the train, Mr. Perkins drove the station wagon up to the front door. Teddy and Babs were on the front seat. They were going to the station to see the twins off. Mrs. Robinson and Joe, the farmhand, were gathered around the wagon to say good-bye to the twins. Grandaddy put their last traveling bag in the wa-

gon. He put the bird cage in and the air gun and the fishing rod.

Grandmother came rushing out of the door. "Here," she said, "don't forget this chocolate cake I baked for your mother. Sarah, be sure to carry it very carefully."

"Mark, you're going without your coat," called Grandaddy.

At last the twins were ready. They kissed everyone good-bye. The wagon started. "Good-bye! Good-bye!" they called.

Everyone waved. "Good-bye, Sarah!" they called. "Good-bye, Mark!"

They hadn't gone very far when Mark cried, "Grandaddy! I forgot my turtle. We'll have to go back for Barney."

Grandaddy turned the car around and drove back to the house. Mark jumped out. He ran into the kitchen. "I forgot my turtle," he shouted.

He picked up the box and in a moment he was back in the wagon.

Off they started again. They had to go all the way into town to the station because the express train didn't stop at the little station nearby. Only the local train stopped there early in the morning.

They drove along the dirt road in a cloud of dust until they turned into the main highway. Jake's gasoline station was on the corner. Jake ran out when he saw the station wagon. He waved wildly. The children waved back. "Good-bye," they called, "Good-bye!"

Jake ran after them, waving. The children waved until they could see him no longer.

The wagon flew over the smooth road. In a few moments a policeman motioned for Mr. Perkins to drive over to the side of the road. Mr. Perkins drew up and stopped the wagon.

"Is your name Perkins?" asked the officer.

"Yes," said Mr. Perkins.

"Well, you forgot your lunch," said the officer.

Mr. Perkins' mouth dropped open—he was so surprised. "How do you know?" he asked.

"Your wife telephoned Jake at the gas station. She told him to stop you, but you didn't pay any attention to him. Just then, I came along, so he sent me after you."

"Thank you very much," said Mr. Perkins.

Once more he turned the wagon around and started back to the farm.

"He was a nice policeman, wasn't he?" said

Sarah. "It would be terrible to go without our lunch."

"It will be terrible if you miss your train," said Grandaddy.

He drove as fast as he could over the dirt road. As they swung into the drive, Grandmother came running to meet them. She handed the lunch box to Teddy, and Grandaddy turned the wagon around. Back they went to the highway. Grandaddy looked at his watch. "We'll never make the train," he said. "You'll miss it as sure as my name is Perkins."

"Oh, Grandaddy!" cried Sarah. "What shall we do?"

"There is nothing to do but go to the little station where they load the milk and see if we can flag the train."

"Do you think the train will stop?" asked Teddy.

"I don't know for sure, but we can try it," said Grandaddy.

Mr. Perkins turned into the road that led to the little station. "It's due to pass there in fifteen minutes," he said.

"What shall we use to flag the train, Grandaddy?" asked Sarah.

"I don't know," said Grandaddy. "We ought to have something red."

"I've got red socks on," said Sarah. "I'll take one off." Sarah slipped off her shoe and took off her sock.

When they reached the station, they still had five minutes before the train was due.

"Now, I'll do the waving," said Grandaddy. "You children stand back in the shed where it is safe. After all, the train may go by."

All of a sudden, there was a sharp whistle. "Here it comes!" shouted Grandaddy. Mark could feel himself tingling with excitement. Sarah's knees felt wobbly.

The children ran back to the shed, and Grandaddy ran along beside the track toward the train. He was waving Sarah's sock.

The children could hear the train now, rushing toward them. Then they heard the screech of the brakes, and the train slowed up and stopped at the station. The children rushed forward. A conductor jumped down. Mr. Perkins pushed the children up the steps. Sarah clutched her doll under one arm and held the chocolate cake in the other.

"Mr. Perkins will meet these children at Washington," said Grandaddy, as he handed up all the boxes and bags and packages.

"All right, sir," said the conductor. "Don't worry about them. I'll deliver them to their father. I know these children. I brought them up here in June."

Mark and Sarah stood on the platform with the conductor. The train began to pull away from the station. "Good-bye!" they called. "Good-bye, Grandaddy! Good-bye, Teddy and Babs!"

"Good-bye," shouted Teddy and Babs.

"Good-bye!" called Grandaddy.

In a moment the train was out of sight.

"Oh, Mr. Perkins!" cried Babs, "you forgot to give Sarah her sock."